Through the Eyes of

CHILDREN

MEXICO

Connie Bickman

Published by Abdo & Daughters, 4940 Viking Drive, Suite 622, Edina, Minnesota 55435.

Library bound edition distributed by Rockbottom Books, Pentagon Tower, P.O. Box 36036, Minneapolis, Minnesota 55435.

Printed in the United States.

Cover Photo credit: Connie Bickman
Interior Photo credits: Connie Bickman
Map created by John Hamilton

Edited By Julie Berg

LIBRARY OF CONGRESS CATALOGING-IN-PUBLICATION DATA

Bickman, Connie.
    Children of Mexico / Connie Bickman.
        p.   cm. -- (Through the Eyes of Children)
    Includes index.
    ISBN 1-56239-328-6
    1. Children--Mexico--Social life and customs--Juvenile literature.
    2. Mexico--Social life and customs--Juvenile literature.
    [1. Mexico--Social life and customs.]   I. Title. II. Series.
    F1210.B53   1994
    972--dc20   94-12497
                                              CIP
                                                AC

Contents

Introduction to Mexico

The first people of Mexico were Indians.
They were the Maya, the Toltec, and the Aztec.
They built beautiful pyramids and temples out of stone.
These were used for ceremonies.
You can visit many of these ancient sites today.
You will learn about the history of the people of that time.
Much of their history is written in pictures on the stones.

Mexico is a land of many climates.
It is hot in some places and cool in other areas.
You can climb mountains or swim in the ocean.
You can walk in the desert or hike to a volcano.
Or you can explore a tropical forest and jungle.

Many people like to go to Mexico for a vacation.
Mexico is music, dancing, and bright colors.
It is also filled with exciting people.
Let's see how the children of Mexico live.

MEXICO

Tijuana

Ciudad Juárez

Ensenada

Sonoran Desert

Hermosillo

Rio Grande

Chihuahua

Baja California

Monterrey

La Paz

Sierra Madre

Leon

Guadalajara

Mexico City

Veracruz

Yucatan Peninsula

Acapulco

Oaxaca

Tapachura

750 miles

Population
81.1 million

Area (square miles)
761,604

City Population
● Over 10 million
● Over 2 million
● Over 1 million
○ Under 1 million

Capital: Mexico City

Meet the Children

The children of Mexico come from many
different backgrounds.
Some are Mestizo.
That means they are of mixed cultures.
They could be from Spanish, Portuguese, or
Indian parents.
Some are Aztec, Mixtec and Maya Indian.

The common language in Mexico is Spanish.
There are 31 Indian languages spoken throughout
the country.
Many of the children also speak English.

See the faces of the
children on these pages.
They are all happy faces.

Most of the children
in Mexico have shiny
dark hair.
They have beautiful
faces with large dark
eyes.

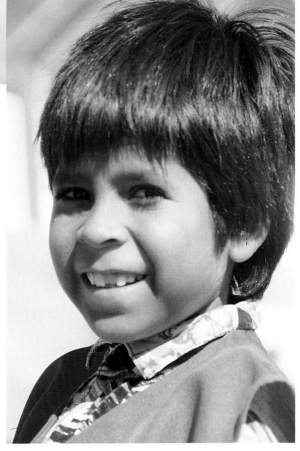

What's Good to Eat?

Tacos, tortillas, enchiladas, and refried beans.
Have you ever eaten any of these?
They are all Mexican food.
But you will find that they taste much different
in Mexico than at home.
All of the food used to make these dishes
comes right from the market.
So the dishes are prepared with fresh food.
Most of the markets are in the open, with
no refrigeration.
The ovens and utensils used to make food is
also different.
But the best thing is that the food is hot
and spicy!

Fishing is important in coastal cities. Shrimp is the largest industry in some areas. You can see how big these jumbo shrimp are. They are served with lime.

This man is
wearing a huge sombrero.
He is serving tamales.
Tamales are meat, rolled in corn meal.
Then they are wrapped in corn husks and steamed.
They taste good.

What Do They Wear?

Children dress a lot like you do.
This girl lives in the city.
She is wearing a pretty new dress.
She is at a birthday party.

This girl lives in the country. She is also wearing a dress. Most young girls in Mexico wear dresses.

Baseball shirts and hats are very popular. This boy's baseball hat has a flag and says "Mexico."

Where Do They Live?

These children live in an area called the Yucatan.
Their houses are huts by the beach.
They are getting water from an outside sink.
They will carry the water to their house for washing.

These boys live in the city of
Puerto Vallarta.
Their homes are the same
as yours.

They like to play basketball on
their school playground.

There are many small villages throughout Mexico.
People here farm and work in the nearby mines.
Houses are built into the side of the hills.

This little girl lives in a rock house.
Her house is over 400 years old.
It has a dirt floor and stone walls.
The big rock next to her is called a matate.
It is used for crushing corn to make food.

The children of this family help their parents with the farming.
They have animals to care for.
They have no electricity or running water.
Their lives are very simple.

Getting Around

Three-wheeled bicycles are very useful in the city.
They help carry groceries and things to sell.
They also help carry the children around.
This boy is collecting things in boxes on his bike.

This boy
likes to
travel
around the countryside.
He rides on his burro or donkey.
The boy's name is Jose.
The burro's name is Pancho Villa.
The burro is Jose's friend.

School is Fun

These boys go to school in an open courtyard.
It is hot most of the time in Mexico, so the children like
to be outside.
They line their desks up in the shade of buildings
to study.
Behind them is the playground.
They study history and math.
They also study Spanish and English.

How Do They Work?

Do you like to play with clay?
This girl does.
She is helping to make clay suns.
Her family makes suns and moons to sell to tourists.
Sometimes the clay is painted bright colors.

Selling jewelry and blankets in the market is big business.
This boy is showing his handmade necklaces.
He will tell you that you can have a special price!

Making bricks is a hard job.
It is done in the open sun, so it is very hot work.
These three boys help to mix mud, straw and other ingredients.
The mixture is poured into molds and dried in the sun.
Many of the buildings in Mexico are made from bricks.

Their Land

These are huge pyramids.
They are the Pyramid of the Sun and the Pyramid of the Moon.
They were built by the Aztec Indians many years ago.
They are part of an ancient city called Teotihuacan—near Mexico City.

Uxmal is
another ancient
site
in Mexico.
It was a huge
city a long
time ago.
Temples and
stone buildings
still remain.
They help us
understand
the history
of Mexico.
The children are
climbing down
the pyramid.

Another ancient
city is Chichen'
Itza'.
It was famous
as a large
spiritual city.
The statue in
front of the
pyramid is called
a choc mol.
It was used
at one time
for Indian ceremonies.
The temples have carvings in their stone walls.
They are of serpents, warriors and animals.
The carvings tell stories of Mexico's history.

Animals Are Friends

Would you like to have an iguana for a pet? An iguana is a type of large lizard. This boy says it is a fun pet to take care of. It looks scary—like a small dinosaur—but it is friendly.

Horses are always good friends.
This boy likes to take care of his horses.
He would even let you ride them along the beach.

Life in the City

A park in the city is called a zocalo.
It is a good meeting place for families and friends.
These two boys are riding their bikes around the zocalo.
They are on their way home from school.

Shopping in
your own
neighborhood
is fun.
Everyone
knows you
and is
friendly.
This girl
is buying
a treat.
Money in
Mexico is called pesos.

Family Living

Many families live in the jungle.
It is important for the children to stay close to their parents.
The jungle could be dangerous if you were lost.

These people are Mayan Indians.
They live in the Yucatan, near
the ocean.
Their house is a grass hut.
They sleep in hammocks to keep
themselves cool.

This brother and his
sisters are on vacation.
They live in the city.
They are having fun
visiting the beach.

What are Traditions?

Colorful art and paintings are part of Mexico's culture.
It is a tradition to paint beautiful pictures on buildings.
Most of the pictures tell of Mexico's history.
This painting is on a store near the girl's house.

Bullfights are an old and
important tradition in Mexico.
It is called the Fiesta Brava.
That means the Brave
Celebration.
This boy is selling posters of
a bullfighter.
The poster is written in Spanish.
The bullfighter is riding a horse.
He is dressed in fancy clothing.
The horse is also decorated.

Just for Fun

Volleyball is a fun sport.
These boys like to play volleyball in the sand.
Do you see their houses behind them?
The roofs are made of palm and grasses.

Children love to play baseball.
These boys are playing baseball
on the beach.
They have a bat and a ball, but
no gloves.
It is hard to run to catch the
ball in the sand.
It is also hard to run the bases.
But if you fall, the sand is soft!

Making mud pies and sand sculptures are fun.
These children like playing at the beach.
They are planning to build a big sand castle.

Children are the Same Everywhere

It is fun to see how children in other countries live. They may play, go to school, and have families just like you. They may work, travel and dress different than you.

But one thing is always the same in every country. That is a smile. If you smile at other children, they will smile back. That is how you make new friends. It's fun to have new friends all over the world!

Glossary

Aztec - Indian people of Mexico.

Burro - Donkey

Chichen' Itza' - Ancient Mayan ceremonial site. The name means "At the mouth of the well of the Water Witch."

Choc mol - Statue used in ancient Mayan ceremonies.

Enchilada - A tortilla dipped in hot sauce, filled with meat, and fried. Served with sauce and cheese.

Fiesta - A festival.

Fiesta Brava - Spanish name for a bullfight meaning "Brave Celebration."

Iguana - A large member of the lizard family.

Maya - Native Indians of the Yucatan.

Matate - Carved out stone used to grind corn and grains.

Mestizo - People from Spanish, Mexican, and Indian parents.

Mixtec - Indian people of Southwest Mexico.

Pesos - Money used in Mexico.

Puerto Vallarta - City in southern coast of Mexico.

Pyramid - A triangle-shaped monument built by the Maya and Aztecs.

Sombrero - A large brimmed hat.

Taco - A tortilla shell filled with meat.

Tamale - Meat, rolled in corn meal, wrapped in corn husks and steamed.

Teotihuacan - An ancient Toltec religious center 34 miles from Mexico City.

Toltec - Indian people of Mexico.

Tortilla - Flat "pancake" made from corn or wheat flour.

Uxmal - Ancient Mayan ceremonial site. The name means "The place of the eternal moon."

Yucatan - A peninsula separating the Gulf of Mexico from the Caribbean. Also one of the states of Mexico.

Zocalo - A family park—usually an entire block in the city.

Index

About the Author/Photographer

Connie Bickman is a photojournalist whose photography has won regional and international awards.

She is retired from a ten-year newspaper career and currently owns her own portrait studio and art gallery. She is an active freelance photographer and writer whose passion is to travel the far corners of the world in search of adventure and the opportunity to photograph native cultures.

She is a member of the National Press Association and the Minnesota Newspaper Photographers Association.